BANSHEES, AND OTHER DEATH WARNINGS

BY

ST. JOHN D. SEYMOUR

Copyright © 2013 Read Books Ltd.
This book is copyright and may not be
reproduced or copied in any way without
the express permission of the publisher in writing

British Library Cataloguing-in-Publication Data
A catalogue record for this book is available from the
British Library

CONTENTS

ST. JOHN D. SEYMOUR 1

BANSHEES, AND OTHER
DEATH-WARNINGS 3

ST. JOHN D. SEYMOUR

St. John Drelincourt Seymour was born in the second half of the 19th century in Ireland. Around 1913, he came to realize that although Ireland was replete with collections of folklore and fairy-tales, the country's rich tradition of ghost stories remained largely untapped. Working with friend Harry L. Neligan, Seymour set out to correct this. The two of them put out a request for anecdotes in the newspapers of the day, and compiled the stories they received in what is now Seymour's most well-known 'non-fiction' work, *True Irish Ghost Stories* (1914). Around the same time, Seymour published his other more popular titles, *Irish Witchcraft and Demonology* and *Haunted Houses in or Near Dublin*.

BANSHEES, AND OTHER DEATH-WARNINGS

OF all Irish ghosts, fairies, or bogles, the Banshee (sometimes called locally the "Bohēēntha" or "Bankēēntha") is the best known to the general public: indeed, cross-Channel visitors would class her with pigs, potatoes, and other fauna and flora of Ireland, and would expect her to make manifest her presence to them as being one of the sights of the country. She is a spirit with a lengthy pedigree—how lengthy no man can say, as its roots go back into the dim, mysterious past. The most famous Banshee of ancient times was that attached to the kingly house of O'Brien, Aibhill, who haunted the rock of Craglea above Killaloe, near the old palace of Kincora. In A.D. 1014 was fought the battle of Clontarf, from which the aged king, Brian Boru, knew that he would never come away alive, for the previous night Aibhill had appeared to him to tell him of his impending fate. The Banshee's method of foretelling death in olden times differed from that adopted by her at the present day: now she wails and wrings her hands, as a general rule, but in the old Irish tales she is to be found washing human heads and limbs, or blood-stained clothes, till the water is all dyed with human blood—this would take place before a battle. So it would seem that in the course of centuries her attributes and characteristics have changed somewhat.

Very different descriptions are given of her personal appearance. Sometimes she is young and beautiful, sometimes old and of a fearsome appearance. One writer describes her as "a tall, thin woman with uncovered head, and long hair that floated round her shoulders, attired in something which seemed either a loose white cloak or a sheet thrown hastily around her, uttering piercing cries". Another person, a coachman, saw her one evening sitting on a stile in the yard; she seemed to be a very small woman, with blue eyes, long light hair, and wearing a red cloak. Other descriptions will be found in this chapter. By the way, it does not seem to be true that the Banshee exclusively follows families of Irish descent, for the last incident had reference to the death of a member of a Co. Galway family English by name and origin.

One of the oldest and best-known Banshee stories is that related in the *Memoirs* of Lady Fanshawe.[1] In 1642 her husband, Sir Richard, and she chanced to visit a friend, the head of an Irish sept, who resided in his ancient baronial castle, surrounded with a moat. At midnight she was awakened by a ghastly and supernatural scream, and looking out of bed, beheld in the moonlight a female face and part of the form hovering at the window. The distance from the ground, as well as the circumstance of the moat, excluded the possibility that what she beheld was of this world. The face was that of a young and rather handsome woman, but pale, and the hair, which was reddish, was loose and dishevelled. The dress, which Lady Fanshawe's terror did not prevent her remarking accurately, was that of the ancient Irish. This apparition continued to exhibit itself for some time, and then vanished with two shrieks similar to that which had first excited Lady Fanshawe's attention. In the morning, with infinite terror, she communicated to her host what she had witnessed, and found him prepared not only to credit, but to account for the superstition. "A near relation of my family," said he, "expired last night in this castle. We disguised our certain expectation of the event from you, lest it should throw a cloud over the cheerful reception which was your due. Now, before such an event happens in this family or castle, the female spectre whom you have seen is always visible. She is believed to be the spirit of a woman of inferior rank, whom one of my ancestors degraded himself by marrying, and whom afterwards, to expiate the dishonour done to his family, he caused to be drowned in the moat." In strictness this woman could hardly be termed a Banshee.

The motive for the haunting is akin to that in the tale of the Scotch "Drummer of Cortachy", where the spirit of the murdered man haunts the family out of revenge, and appears before a death.

The late Mr. T. J. Westropp, M.A., furnished the following story: "My maternal grandmother heard the following tradition from her mother, one of the Miss Ross-Lewins, who witnessed the occurrence. Their father, Mr. Harrison Ross-Lewin, was away in Dublin on law business, and in his absence the young people went off to spend the evening with a friend who lived some miles away. The night was fine and lightsome as they were returning, save at one point where the road ran between trees or high hedges not far to the west of the old church of Kilchrist. The latter, like many similar ruins, was a simple oblong building, with long side-walls and high gables, and at that time it and its graveyard were unenclosed, and lay in the open fields. As the party passed down the long dark lane they suddenly heard in the distance loud keening and clapping of hands, as the country-people were accustomed to do when lamenting the dead. The Ross-Lewins hurried on, and came in sight of the church, on the side wall of which a little grey-haired old woman, clad in a dark cloak, was running to and fro, chanting and wailing, and throwing up her arms. The girls were very frightened, but the young men ran forward and surrounded the ruin, and two of them went into the church, the apparition vanishing from the wall as they did so. They searched every nook, and found no one, nor did any one pass out. All were now well scared, and got home as fast as possible. On reaching their home their mother opened the door, and at once told them that she was in terror about their father, for, as she sat looking out the window in the moonlight, a huge raven with fiery eyes lit on the sill, and tapped three times on the glass. They told her their story, which only added to their anxiety, and as they stood talking, taps came to the nearest window, and they saw the bird again. A few days later news reached them that Mr. Ross-Lewin had died suddenly in Dublin. This occurred about 1776."

Mr. Westropp also writes that the sister of a former Roman Catholic Bishop told his sisters that when she was a little girl she went out one evening with some other children for a walk. Going down the road, they passed the gate of the principal demesne near the town. There was a rock, or large stone, beside the road, on which they saw something. Going nearer, they perceived it to be a little, dark, old woman, who began crying and clapping her hands. Some of them attempted to speak to her, but got frightened, and all finally ran home as quickly as they could. Next day the news came that the gentleman, near whose gate the Banshee had cried, was dead, and it was found on inquiry that he had died at the very hour at which the children had seen the spectre.

A lady who is a relation of one of the compilers, and a member of a Co. Cork family of English descent, sends the two following experiences of a Banshee in her family. "My mother, when a young girl, was standing looking out of the window in their house at Blackrock, near Cork. She suddenly saw a white figure standing on a bridge which was easily visible from the house. The figure waved her arms towards the house, and my mother heard the bitter wailing of the Banshee. It lasted some seconds, and then the figure disappeared. Next morning my grandfather was walking as usual into the city of Cork. He accidentally fell, hit his head against the curbstone, and never recovered consciousness.

"In March 1900 my mother was very ill, and one evening the nurse and I were with her arranging her bed. We suddenly heard the most extraordinary wailing, which seemed to come in waves round and under her bed. We naturally looked everywhere to try and find the cause, but in vain. The nurse and I looked at one another, but made no remark, as my mother did not seem to hear it. My sister was downstairs sitting with my father. She heard it, and thought some terrible thing had happened to her little boy, who was in bed upstairs. She rushed up, and found him sleeping quietly. My father did not hear it. In the house next door they heard it, and ran downstairs, thinking something had happened to the servant; but the latter at once said to them, 'Did you hear the Banshee? Mrs. P. must be dying.' "

A few years ago (*i.e.* before 1894) a curious incident occurred in a public school in connection with the belief in the Banshee. One of the boys, happening to become ill, was at once placed in a room by himself, where he used to sit all day. On one occasion, as he was being visited by the doctor, he suddenly started up from his seat, and affirmed that he heard somebody crying. The doctor, of course, who could hear or see nothing, came to the conclusion that the illness had slightly affected his brain. However, the boy, who appeared quite sensible, still persisted that he heard some one crying, and furthermore said, "It is the Banshee, as I have heard it before." The following morning the headmaster received a telegram saying that the boy's brother had been accidentally shot dead.[1]

That the Banshee is not confined within the geographical limits of Ireland, but that she can follow the fortunes of a family abroad, and there foretell their death, is clearly shown by the following story. A party of visitors were gathered together on the deck of a private yacht on one of the Italian lakes, and during a lull in the conversation one of them, a Colonel, said to the owner, "Count, who's that queer-looking woman you have on board?" The Count replied that there was nobody except the ladies present and the stewardess, but the speaker protested that he was correct, and suddenly, with a scream of horror, he placed his hands before his eyes and exclaimed, "Oh, my God, what a face!" For some time he was overcome with terror, and at length reluctantly looked up and cried:

"Thank Heavens, it's gone!"

"What was it?" asked the Count.

"Nothing human," replied the Colonel—"nothing belonging to this world. It was a woman of no earthly type, with a queer-shaped, gleaming face, a mass of red hair, and eyes that would have been beautiful but for their expression, which was hellish. She had on a green hood, after the fashion of an Irish peasant."

An American lady present suggested that the description tallied with that of the Banshee, upon which the Count said:

"I am an O'Neill—at least I am descended from one. My family name is, as you know, Neilsini, which, little more than a century ago, was O'Neill. My great-grandfather served in the Irish Brigade, and on its dissolution at the time of the French Revolution had the good fortune to escape the general massacre of officers, and in company with an O'Brien and a Maguire fled across the frontier and settled in Italy. On his death his son, who had been born in Italy, and was far more Italian than Irish, changed his name to

Banshees, and other Death Warnings

Neilsini, by which name the family has been known ever since. But for all that we are Irish."

"The Banshee was yours, then!" ejaculated the Colonel. "What exactly does it mean?"

"It means," the Count replied solemnly, "the death of some one very nearly associated with me. Pray Heaven it is not my wife or daughter."

On that score, however, his anxiety was speedily removed, for within two hours he was seized with a violent attack of angina pectoris, and died before morning.[1]

Mr. Elliott O'Donnell, to whose article on "Banshees" we are indebted for the above, adds: "The Banshee never manifests itself to the person whose death it is prognosticating. Other people may see or hear it, but the fated one never, so that when every one present is aware of it but one, the fate of that one may be regarded as pretty well certain."

We must now pass on from the subject of Banshees to the kindred one of "Headless Coaches", the belief in which is widespread through the country. Apparently these dread vehicles must be distinguished from the phantom coaches, of which numerous circumstantial tales are also told. The first are harbingers of death, and in this connection are very often attached to certain families; the latter appear to be spectral phenomena pure and simple, whose appearance does not necessarily portend evil or death.

"At a house in Co. Limerick," writes Mr. T. J. Westropp, "occurred the remarkably attested apparition of the headless coach in June 1806, when Mr. Ralph Westropp, my great-grandfather, lay dying. The story was told by his sons, John, William, and Ralph, to their respective children, who told it to me. They had sent for the doctor, and were awaiting his arrival in the dusk. As they sat on the steps they suddenly heard a heavy rumbling, and saw a huge dark coach drive into the paved court before the door. One of them went down to meet the doctor, but the coach swept past him, and drove down the avenue, which went straight between the fences and hedges to a gate. Two of the young men ran after the coach, which they could hear rumbling before them, and suddenly came full tilt against the avenue gate. The noise had stopped, and they were surprised at not finding the carriage. The gate proved to be locked, and when they at last awoke the lodge-keeper he showed them the keys under his pillow. The doctor arrived a little later, but could do nothing, and the sick man died a few hours afterwards."

Two other good stories come from Co. Clare. One night in April 1821, two servants were sitting up to receive a son of the family, Cornelius O'Callaghan, who had travelled in vain for his health, and was returning home. One of them, Halloran, said that the heavy rumble of a coach roused them. The other servant, Burke, stood on the top of the long flight of steps with a lamp, and sent Halloran down to open the carriage door. He reached out his hand to do so, saw a skeleton looking out, gave one yell, and fell in a heap. When the badly scared Burke picked himself up there was no sign or sound of any coach. A little later the invalid arrived, so exhausted that he died suddenly in the early morning.

On the night of December 11, 1876, a servant of the Macnamaras was going his rounds at Ennistymon, a beautiful spot in a wooded glen, with a broad stream falling in a series of cascades. In the dark he heard the rumbling of wheels on the back avenue, and, knowing from the hour and place that no mortal vehicle could be coming, concluded that it was the death coach, and ran on, opening the gates before it. He had just time to open the third gate, and throw himself on his face beside it, when he heard a coach go clanking past. On the following day Admiral Sir Burton Macnamara died in London.

Mr. Westropp writes that at sight or sound of this coach all gates should be thrown open, and then it will not stop at the house to call for a member of the family, but will only foretell the death of some relative at a distance. We hope our readers will carefully bear in mind this simple method of averting fate.

We may conclude this chapter with some account of strange and varied death-warnings, which are attached to certain families and foretell the coming of the King of Terrors.

In a Co. Wicklow family a death is preceded by the appearance of a spectre; the doors of the sitting-room open and a lady dressed in white satin walks across the room and hall. Before any member of a certain Queen's Co. family died a looking-glass was broken; while in a branch of that family the portent was the opening and shutting of the avenue gate. In another Queen's Co. family, approaching death was heralded by the cry of the cuckoo, no matter at what season of the year it might occur. A Mrs. F. and her son lived near Clonaslee. One day, in mid-winter, their servant heard a cuckoo; they went out for a drive, the trap jolted over a stone, throwing Mrs. F. out, and breaking her neck. The ringing of all the house-bells is another portent which seems to be attached to several families. In another the æolian harp is heard at or before death; an account of this was given to the present writer by a clergyman, who declares that he heard it in the middle of the night when one of his relatives passed away. A death-warning in the shape of a white owl follows the Westropp family. This last appeared, it is said, before a death in 1909, but, as our correspondent remarks, it would be more convincing if it appeared at places where the white owl does *not* nest and fly out every night. No doubt this list might be drawn out to much greater length.

Banshees, and other Death Warnings

In front of the residence of the G. family in Co. Galway there is, or formerly was, a round ring of grass surrounded by a low evergreen hedge. The lady who related this story to our informant stated that one evening dinner was kept waiting for Mr. G., who was absent in town on some business. She went out on the hall-door steps in order to see if the familiar trot of the carriage horses could be heard coming down the road. It was a bright moonlight night, and as she stood there she heard a child crying with a peculiar whining cry, and distinctly saw a small childlike figure running round and round the grass ring inside the evergreen hedge, and casting a shadow in the moonlight. Going into the house she casually mentioned this as a peculiar circumstance to Mrs. G., upon which, to her great surprise, that lady nearly fainted, and got into a terrible state of nervousness. Recovering a little, she told her that this crying and figure were always heard and seen whenever any member met with an accident or before a death. A messenger was immediately sent to meet Mr. G., who was found lying senseless on the road, as the horses had taken fright and bolted, flinging him out and breaking the carriage-pole.

A woman in white follows the family of Coplen Langford, of Kilcosgriff Castle, Co. Limerick, and manifests herself when any member is about to die. The traditional account of her origin, as well as of some of the occasions on which she appeared, have been furnished to the present writer by Mr. Richard Coplen Langford, J.P., of Kilcosgriff.

Over two hundred years ago William Langford, a young man who was in the Army, returned suddenly on leave to Kikosgriff, and finding that the house was full of guests declared that he would sleep in what was then known as the Haunted Chamber. When retiring for the night he placed a pair of pistols on a small table beside his bed, thinking that some one might try to play a practical joke on him, in which event he would give the intruders a good fright. About midnight, when he was going to sleep, he saw the door open slowly, and a lady clad in her night attire, and carrying a lighted candle, enter the room. He pretended to be asleep, but watched her through his half-closed eyelids, and perceived that she had a magnificent diamond ring on her hand. She came slowly to his bedside, bent over and looked at him, then turning down the clothes, got into bed beside him and extinguished the light. He gently put his hand out and touched the hand on which sparkled the ring. He found it, as he had expected, warm flesh and blood; the lady was one of the guests, and was given to walking in her sleep. So he took the ring off her finger, and put it on one of his own. After a very short time she got up, relit the candle, and walked out of the room.

Next morning Mr. Langford came down to the breakfast-room, where all the guests were assembled. While eating his breakfast he displayed the ring somewhat ostentatiously; on catching sight of it sparkling on his finger a young lady, who was a stranger to him, was seized with faintness and had to leave the table. After breakfast, as Mr. Langford was sitting on a seat outside the hall door, the same lady came to him and said:

"Will you tell me where you got that ring? I recognise it as mine, but surely you did not dare to come into my room and take it!"

"Most certainly I did not," he replied. "But to tell you the exact truth *you* came into *my* room, and into my bed, and it was then that I took it off your pretty hand. Take it back," he added. "And when you are doing so you may as well take me with it!" Blushingly she said yes to his unusual method of proposal, and so they were married and lived happily. She was Miss Gertrude St. Ledger, sister to the first Viscount Doneraile, and married William Langford in 1703. When she was dying she told her husband that she would be seen when a death was about to take place in the family.

Such is the tradition, briefly told, of the origin of the White Lady. Our correspondent, Mr. Richard Langford, sends the account of four of her appearances, three of which he witnessed himself.

"My father told me that one night a black setter dog of his

got up on one of the piers of the yard-gate and commenced to howl most dismally. He went out to it in his nightgown, but could not get it to come down. Suddenly he saw a woman walk across the yard; he called out to her, but she returned no answer, and walked on till she went through a door into a stable. He followed her, but found nothing there except the horse. He returned to bed, but the dog continued howling all night, and in the morning he learnt of the death of his father at Miltown Malbay. This occurred in September 1856.

"When the latter's wife, my grandmother, died, I was in the dining-room here, and heard a most unearthly crying in the deer-park. I called to my brother, who was in the nursery (as we termed a certain room) to come and listen; as soon as he came it stopped, so he went away laughing at me. It soon commenced again, and on looking out of the window I saw a white figure move along a path by the garden, which is called the Lovers' Walk. It was then getting fairly dark. I was startled somewhat, but called out, whereupon the figure disappeared in a clump of laurels. I went out after it, and carefully examined the spot, but could find no trace of any one. That night my grandmother died.

"In 1889, during my father's last illness I was sitting in the dining-room with no society save that of the family portraits. My father's room was at the end of a long passage; he would have no nurse, and we all had to look after him. I heard a movement outside the dining-room door, so I went and looked out. I was about to walk to see how my father was, when suddenly the white figure of a woman glided by me. I followed her, but she vanished, so I hastened to my father's room, only to find that he had just breathed his last.

"My youngest brother, Crawford Langford of Glenville, had been in failing health for some time, and had gone to Dublin to consult doctors. On his return he was invited by my cousin, Major Langford, D.S.O., of The Abbey, Rathkeale, to go and stay there with him for a few days' change. While there he got worse, and the doctor said it would not be safe to move him. He had two nurses in attendance. On the evening of February 1, 1914, I with one of the nurses was sitting in his room at the Abbey at five o'clock. Tea was announced, so I said to the nurse, 'You go down and have tea, and I shall remain here.' I was seated with my back towards the fire-place on a lounge opposite to the sick man's bed. Suddenly the door opened, and a tall figure of a lady in white walked or rather glided into the room. She went over to my brother's bed, put her arm across him, smiled at him, then looked at me and smiled, and then vanished. I wished to speak to her, but my powers of utterance failed me. My brother died six days later."

A lady correspondent states that her cousin, a Sir Patrick

Dun's nurse, was attending a case in the town of Wicklow. Her patient was a middle-aged woman, the wife of a well-to-do shopkeeper. One evening the nurse was at her tea in the dining-room beneath the sick-room, when suddenly she heard a tremendous crash overhead. Fearing her patient had fallen out of bed, she hurried upstairs, to find her dozing quietly, and there was not the least sign of any disturbance. A member of the family, to whom she related this, told her calmly that that noise was always heard in their house before the death of any of them, and that it was a sure sign that the invalid would not recover. Contrary to the nurse's expectations, she died the following day.

Knocking on the door is another species of death-warning. The Rev. D. B. Knox writes: "On the evening before the wife of a clerical friend of mine died, the knocker of the hall door was loudly rapped. All in the room heard it. The door was opened, but there was no one there. Again the knocker was heard, but no one was to be seen when the door was again opened. A young man, brother of the dying woman, went into the drawing-room and looked through one of the drawing-room windows. The full light of the moon fell on the door, and as he looked the knocker was again lifted and loudly rapped."

Another somewhat similar story was related by a lady who is well known to the present writer, but who, for family reasons, does not wish to have her name published.

"Some years ago my husband and I lived in a residential suburb in Dublin. As our house was a large one we shared it with my husband's father and mother. One winter—I cannot remember if it was before or after Christmas—my mother-in-law was ill, though she did not die until the following summer. My husband and I were sitting by the dining-room fire in the evening, when there came a loud knocking at the hall door. As the maid was out for the evening, I went and opened the door myself, but found no one outside. As this was a quiet residential district, and as the houses were separated from the road by gardens, I knew that it could not be mischievous children giving a 'run-away knock'. Somewhat mystified I returned to the dining-room, and told my husband. He at once replied, 'That is the knocking that follows the family whenever a death is about to occur!'

"My mother-in-law died the following July. In the interval between her death and burial, I heard knocking at the door. I went to open it, thinking of course that some friends or relations were coming in, but to my surprise I found no one on the door-step; and, what was still more peculiar, the crape-covered knocker was up, as if some one were about to complete a knock. I did not see it fall, however, while I was there, nor was there any further knocking. I told some of my people-in-law who were in the house at the time, and they too said that it was the knocking that followed the family."

The following portent occurs in a Co. Cork family. At one time the lady of the house lay ill, and her two daughters were aroused one night by screams proceeding from their mother's room. They rushed in, and found her sitting up in bed, staring at some object unseen to them, but which, from the motion of her eyes, appeared to be moving across the floor. When she became calm she told them, what they had not known before, that members of the family were sometimes warned of the death, or approaching death, of some other member by the appearance of a ball of fire, which would pass slowly through the room; this phenomenon she had just witnessed. A day or two afterwards the mother heard of the death of her brother, who lived in the Colonies.

A strange appearance, known as the "Scanlan lights", is connected with the family of Scanlan of Ballyknockane, Co. Limerick, and is seen frequently at the death of a member. The traditional origin of the lights is connected with a well-known Irish legend, which we give here briefly. Scanlan Mor (died A.D. 640), King of Ossory, from whom the family claim descent, was suspected of disaffection by Aedh mac Ainmire, Ard-Righ of Ireland, who cast him into prison, and loaded him with fetters. When St. Columcille attended the Synod of Drom Ceat, he besought Aedh to free his captive, but the Ard-Righ churlishly refused; whereupon Columcille declared that he should be freed, and that that very night he should unloose his (the Saint's) brogues. Columcille went away, and that night a bright pillar of fire appeared in the air, and hung over the house where Scanlan was imprisoned. A beam of light darted into the room where he lay, and a voice called to him, bidding him rise, and shake off his fetters. In amazement he did so, and was led out past his guards by an angel. He made his way to Columcille, with whom he was to continue that night, and as the Saint stooped down to unloose his brogues Scanlan anticipated him, as he had prophesied.[1]

Such appears to be the traditional origin of the "Scanlan lights". Our correspondent adds: "These are always seen at the demise of a member of the family. We have ascertained that by the present head of the family (Scanlan of Ballyknockane) they were seen, first, as a pillar of fire with radiated crown at the top; and secondly, inside the house, by the room being lighted up brightly in the night. By other members of the family now living these lights have been seen in the shape of balls of fire of various sizes." The above was copied from a private manuscript written some few years ago. Our correspondent further states: "I also have met with four persons in this county [Limerick] who have seen the lights on Knockfierna near Ballyknockane before the death of a Scanlan, one of the four being the late head of the family and owner, William Scanlan, J.P., who saw the flames on the hill-side on the day of his aunt's death some years ago. The last occasion was as late as 1913, on the eve of the death of a Scanlan related to the present owner of Ballyknockane."

But of all the death-warnings in connection with Irish families surely the strangest is the Gormanstown foxes. The crest of that noble family is a running fox, while the same animal also forms one of the supporters of the coat-of-arms. The story is, that when the head of the house is dying the foxes—not spectral foxes, but creatures of flesh and blood—leave the coverts and congregate at Gormanstown Castle.

Let us see what proof there is of this. When Jenico, the 12th Viscount, was dying in 1860, foxes were seen about the house and moving towards the house for some days previously. Just before his death three foxes were playing about and making a noise close to the house, and just in front of the "cloisters", which are yew-trees planted and trained in that shape. The Hon. Mrs. Farrell states as regards the same that the foxes came in pairs into the demesne, and sat under the Viscount's bedroom window, and barked and howled all night. Next morning they were to be found crouching about in the grass in front and around the house. They walked through the poultry and never touched them. After the funeral they disappeared.

At the death of Edward, the 13th Viscount, in 1876, the

foxes were also there. He had been rather better one day, but the foxes appeared, barking under the window, and he died that night contrary to expectation.

On October 28, 1907, Jenico, the 14th Viscount, died in Dublin. About 8 o'clock that night the coachman and gardener saw two foxes near the chapel (close to the house), five or six more round the front of the house, and several crying in the "cloisters". Two days later the Hon. Richard Preston, R.F.A., was watching by his father's body in the above chapel. About 3 A.M. he became conscious of a slight noise, which seemed to be that of a number of people walking stealthily around the chapel on the gravel walk. He went to the side door, listened, and heard outside a continuous and insistent snuffling or sniffing noise, accompanied by whimperings and scratchings at the door. On opening it he saw a full-grown fox sitting on the path within four feet of him. Just in the shadow was another, while he could hear several more moving close by in the darkness. He then went to the end door, opposite the altar, and on opening it saw two more foxes, one so close that he could have touched it with his foot. On shutting the door the noise continued till 5 A.M., when it suddenly ceased.[1]

[1] Scott's *Lady of the Lake*, notes to Canto III. (edition of 1811). A much better version of the story is to be found in H. C. Fanshawe, *Memoirs of Ann, Lady Fanshawe* (p. 57).

[1] A. G. Bradley, *Notes on some Irish Superstitions*, p. 9.

[1] *Occult Review* for September 1913.

[1] Canon Carrigan, in his *History of tie Diocese of Ossory* (I. 32 intro.), shows that this legend should rather be connected with Scanlan son of Ceannfaeladh.

[1] *New Ireland Review* for April 1908, by permission of the publishers, Messrs. Sealy, Bryers & Walker.

www.ingramcontent.com/pod-product-compliance
Lightning Source LLC
LaVergne TN
LVHW012010260326
834688LV00057B/436